LEVEL 2 READER

# Hot Rod Hamster

## AND THE WACKY WHATEVER RACE!

By **Cynthia Lord**

Cover illustration by **Derek Anderson**

Interior illustrations by **Greg Paprocki**

SCHOLASTIC INC.

To my teacher Mrs. Keitt, who taught me to love reading.—C. L.

For Grace, Marijka, and our entire racing team at Scholastic.—D. A.

Text copyright © 2014 by Cynthia Lord
Illustrations copyright © 2014 by Derek Anderson

LIBRARY OF CONGRESS CATALOGING-IN-PUBLICATION DATA
Lord, Cynthia, author.
Hot Rod Hamster and the Wacky Whatever Race! / by Cynthia Lord ; pictures based on the artwork of Derek Anderson ; interior illustrations by Greg Paprocki . — First edition.   pages cm
Summary: Hot Rod Hamster enlists the help of his friend Dog to build a super sleek soap box racer for the Wacky Whatever Race.
ISBN 978-0-545-69442-1 (hardcover : alk. paper) — ISBN 978-0-545-62678-1 (pbk. : alk. paper)
1. Hamsters—Juvenile fiction. 2. Coaster cars—Juvenile fiction. 3. Racing—Juvenile fiction.
4. Friendship—Juvenile fiction. [1. Hamsters—Fiction. 2. Coaster cars—Fiction. 3. Racing—Fiction.
4. Friendship—Fiction.] I. Anderson, Derek, 1969– illustrator. II. Paprocki, Greg, illustrator.
III. Title.  PZ7.L87734Hov 2014  813.6—dc23  2013046940

10 9 8 7 6 5 4                    17 18 19 20/0

Printed in the U.S.A.            40
This edition first printing, September 2014

The display type was set in Ziggy ITC and Coop Black.
The text was set in Cochin Medium and Gill Sans Bold.
The interior art was created digitally by Greg Paprocki.
Art direction and book design by Marijka Kostiw

**Hot Rod Hamster** was on his way to the junkyard to see his friend Dog.

But as he passed the auto shop, something made him stop.

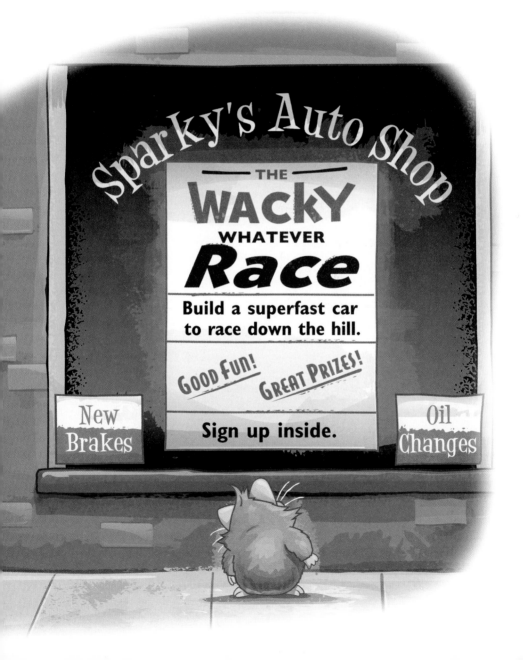

Sparky's Auto Shop

THE
**WACKY**
WHATEVER
*Race*

Build a superfast car
to race down the hill.

Good Fun!    Great Prizes!

Sign up inside.

New Brakes

Oil Changes

# RULES FOR THE
# WACKY
## WHATEVER
# Race

1. The car must be made from a box.
2. It must have four wheels.
3. No motors are allowed. Each car will get only one push at the starting line to help it roll down the hill.
4. During the race, the driver's paws cannot touch the ground. Only the car's wheels can touch the ground.
5. The first car to roll across the finish line will be the winner.

Long box.

Tall box.

**Which would *you* choose?**

Dog finds some tools,
and Hamster cuts a door.
Mice tape and glue.
Be careful where you pour!

Fat wheels.

Slow wheels.

**Which would *you* choose?**

Dog finds wheel rods,
and Hamster drills a hole.
Mice bring the wheels.
One is on a roll!

Hot flames.

Cold flames.

Pink flames.

Gold flames.

**Which would *you* choose?**

Dog brings some paint,
and Hamster opens cans.
Mice stir and mix.
Lots of pretty pans!

Dog gives a push, and . . .

. . . Hamster's in the lead!

Mice gasp and groan.
Hamster's losing speed!

Dog points and shouts.
Cars are coming fast!
Mice hide their eyes.
Hamster will be last.

As soon as Hot Rod Hamster's paws touch the ground, he will be out of the race.

Dog shakes his head.
Poor Hamster really tried.

Mice stare and gasp
as Hamster climbs inside!

**Can Hot Rod Hamster win the race?**